The Queen's
Dragon

First published in 2002 by
Franklin Watts
96 Leonard Street
London
EC2A 4XD

Franklin Watts Australia
45–51 Huntley Street
Alexandria
NSW 2015

Text © Anne Cassidy 2002
Illustration © Gwyneth Williamson 2002

A CIP catalogue record for this book is available
from the British Library.

ISBN 0 7496 4472 9 (hbk)
ISBN 0 7496 4618 7 (pbk)

Series Editor: Louise John
Series Advisor: Dr Barrie Wade
Cover Design: Jason Anscomb
Design: Peter Scoulding

Printed in China

The Queen's
Dragon

by Anne Cassidy and Gwyneth Williamson

W
FRANKLIN WATTS
LONDON • SYDNEY

The Queen was fed up with her dragon, Harry.

"You're old," she said. "You're too fat. Your skin has lost its shine. And your wings are too floppy!"

Harry hid behind the Queen's throne. He closed his eyes and sighed. He put his claws over his ears. He didn't want to hear.

The Queen shouted at the top of her voice: "Your fire has gone out! You're no good to me any more!"

10

And with that, the Queen decided
to find a new dragon.

Harry was sad. His friend, the parrot, flew round the room.

He landed on Harry's head.

"Never mind, Harry," he
squawked. "Don't cry!"

The Queen sent for some new dragons. A red one with graceful wings arrived, then a blue one with a sleek tail.

But the Queen was jealous – the
dragons were just too beautiful.
"These dragons are no good!" she
yelled. "Get me some others!"

Harry ran outside. He was
so upset. The parrot
felt sorry for him.
"Poor Harry,
poor Harry!"
he squawked.

17

The parrot decided to help Harry

to get fit. They started running.

They played tennis.

They went swimming.

The next day, two more tiny dragons arrived at the castle for the Queen. They had wings like silk and flew daintily from tree to tree.

"These dragons are too small!" shouted the Queen. "Get me some others!"

In the meantime, the parrot helped Harry to polish his scales.

He gave Harry breathing lessons.

Soon, Harry's fire was

hot and fierce.

The Queen was grumpy. Another dragon arrived at the castle. It was like a giant snake with wings.

The dragon wrapped itself around the Queen on her throne. "Help me!" she yelled. "This dragon is too scary. Take it away at once!"

Harry was looking great. The parrot was pleased. "Pretty boy, pretty boy!" he squawked.

The Queen saw Harry and was astonished. "Is that my Harry?" she asked.

Harry stood tall and roared.
His flames curled into the air.
His wings were straight and his
scales were shiny. He was a very
handsome dragon indeed.

"I've changed my mind," said
the Queen, happily. "I'm not going
to get a new dragon after all."
Harry and the parrot were
delighted – but only for a moment...

"I think I might get a new parrot instead," sniggered the Queen.

Hopscotch has been specially designed to fit the requirements of the National Literacy Strategy. It offers real books by top authors and illustrators for children developing their reading skills.

There are five other Hopscotch stories to choose from:

Marvin, the Blue Pig
Written by Karen Wallace, illustrated by Lisa Williams
Marvin is the only blue pig on the farm. He tries hard to make himself pink but nothing seems to work. Then, one day, his friend Esther gives him some advice...

Plip and Plop
Written by Penny Dolan, illustrated by Lisa Smith
Plip and Plop are two pesky pigeons that live in Sam's grandpa's garden. And if anyone went out, Plip and Plop got busy... Sam has to think of a way to get rid of them!

Flora McQuack
Written by Penny Dolan, illustrated by Kay Widdowson
Flora McQuack finds a lost egg by the side of the loch and decides to hatch it. But when the egg cracks open, Flora is in for a surprise!

Naughty Nancy
Written by Anne Cassidy, illustrated by Desideria Guicciardini
Norman's little sister Nancy is the naughtiest girl he knows. When Mum goes out for the day, Norman tries hard to keep Nancy out of trouble, but things don't quite go according to plan!

Willie the Whale
Written by Joy Oades, illustrated by Barbara Vagnozzi
Willie the Whale decides to go on a round-the-world adventure – from the South Pole to the desert and even to New York. But is the city really the place for a big, friendly whale?